# Beans on Toast

# Beans on Toast

Shelley Hrdlitschka

ORCA BOOK PUBLISHERS

**Canadian Cataloguing in Publication Data**
Hrdlitschka, Shelley, 1956–
Beans on toast

ISBN 1-55143-116-5

I. Title.
PS8565.R44B42 1998   jC813'.54   C97–911117-X
PZ7.H855Be 1998


**Library of Congress Catalog Card Number:** 97-81070


Orca Book Publishers gratefully acknowledges the support of our
publishing programs provided by the following agencies: the
Department of Canadian Heritage, The Canada Council for the Arts,
and the British Columbia Ministry Arts Council.


Cover design by Christine Toller
Cover and interior illustrations by Ljuba Levstek
Printed and bound in Canada


Orca Book Publishers          Orca Book Publishers
PO Box 5626, Station B        PO Box 468
Victoria, BC  Canada          Custer, WA   USA
V8R 6S4                       98240-0468


00  99  98   5  4  3  2  1

*In memory of Dad and to Mom —*
*for making Band Camp,*
*and so much else, possible.*

# Chapter One

Madison felt invisible as she entered Spruce Hall. Lunch was in full swing. The tables were crowded and the eighty-five teenagers were talking and laughing. No one acknowledged her late arrival. She picked up a plate and filled it with raw vegetables and an egg salad sandwich. She chose a carton of milk. Now for the hard part. She hesitated, braced herself, then turned to survey the crowded room. By arriving late she had hoped that some of the campers would have left, leaving a table free. But no tables were empty, and no one was smiling at her, beckoning to her to join them. She looked for an available chair. There was one at a table filled with senior boys. Luke was there. There was no way she could join them. She spotted the girls from her cabin. There wasn't a free chair at their table, but there was space for her to put one there. Her cabin mates glanced at her as she pulled a chair up and sat down, but immediately redirected their attention to Danica, who was flushed with excitement.

"He came up behind me and pushed me in the pool," she continued. "That's the second time this week! Do you think it *means* anything?"

"It means he's a jerk and likes pushing people in the pool." Ashley was good at putting people in their place. Madison smiled to herself. Danica needed a reality check now and again.

"No. I've got this feeling about him. You know how you just *know* when someone likes you?" Danica flipped a long coil of permed black hair from one side of her face to the other. It fell forward and she tilted her head to keep it out of her eyes.

"Why don't we just ask him?" teased Alicia. She searched the room, pretending to be looking for Jake. It was well known among the girls in Cabin Five that Danica liked him. Danica reached across the table and grabbed Alicia's arm.

"Don't you dare!" she hissed. "You know the rule. We all know who each other likes, so no one can blab. If you blab, Alicia, I'll tell Tyler you like him."

"I'm only kidding," laughed Alicia. "Let me go." She pulled her sunburned and freckled arm free of Danica's grip.

The girls began to pick up their dishes and head toward the kitchen. Madison avoided their eyes, but she didn't expect them to wait for her. She ate her lunch, feeling more invisible than ever. Although she shared the same cabin as these girls, she was not included as one of them. No one had ever asked her who she liked. No one cared.

There was a rest period from 1:00 to 2:00 every afternoon during which the campers were supposed to read, write letters or nap. Madison slowly trudged back to the cabin after lunch. She knew she'd find the girls in her cabin doing the usual—discussing boys and swapping stories. She would have loved to join the conversation, sharing all the things she found exciting about Luke, but she didn't know how to break in—how to get started. These girls had been in band together for a long time. She was the only new girl. She pulled a book out of her knapsack and flopped on her bed instead. As she stared at the words, her mind floated back to the day she picked the book out at the library. The conversation in the cabin became background noise, and Madison could hear her mother's voice as it sounded in the library that day.

"You won't need more than a couple books at Band Camp, honey. You'll be having so much fun that there won't be time to read."

"Don't be so sure," was Madison's sulky reply.

"Well, with that attitude of course you won't." Madison could hear her mother's voice rise in pitch the way it did when she was getting annoyed. "I don't know what's the matter with you, Madi. I've spent a fortune that I don't have on flute lessons for you. You could at least act a little grateful. Band Camp will give you intense practice time and you'll get to know some of the other girls, too. It's about time you started joining in. It has been almost a year since we moved here and you still lie around sulking. It's time you accepted your situation and got on with life."

Madison saw the librarian glance at them as her mother's voice got louder and higher. She quickly selected two more books and took them to the checkout counter. As they headed across the parking lot toward the bus stop, her mother continued talking.

"Your dad's as fed up with you as I am. He told me that you haven't written him in over a month. He says you don't try to make conversation when he phones on Sunday nights."

"Why can't I go to Dad's instead of Band Camp? It wouldn't cost as much!"

"Damn it, Madison. We've been over this a million times. Your dad hasn't got the time to spend with you during the summer. It's his peak business time. You're going to see him at Christmas."

"But the kids in band don't like me!"

"They would like you just fine if you'd make an effort to be friendly. I've watched you. You hide behind all that hair and stare at your feet. How can they know whether they like you or not if you don't let them get to know you?" Madison noticed her mother's voice becoming lower in pitch and sounding a little softer. It had taken her mother quite awhile to make new friends, too.

The bonging of a bass drum pulled Madison back to the present. Rest time was over and the campers were free until their afternoon band practice. The other girls leapt off their bunks, continuing their conversations as they headed out the cabin door.

Madison walked slowly to the concession. Being alone in free time was even worse than at mealtime, she thought. She bought a bag of chips and munched them as she wandered around the camp, watching the activities that everyone else seemed to be involved in. The tennis and badminton courts were full. She walked past the horseshoe pit and the basketball court and down the bank to the beach. She sank down in the sand and leaned against a log. Maybe she would blend in with the sand and no one would notice she was alone. Still.

"Hi, Madison!" came a friendly voice from behind her. She turned her head and smiled at Lisa, their band director. "Can I join you?"

"Sure." Madison liked Lisa, but she knew Lisa was just feeling sorry for her. Why else would she want to hang out?

"Want a chip?" asked Madison.

"Sure. Thanks." They sat quietly for a few minutes, watching a group of campers swimming in the enclosed area of water they called "the pool." It was actually a rectangular wooden deck anchored a few meters off the beach. The lifeguard was pacing the deck, blowing his whistle whenever the waterplay became too rough.

Lisa finally broke the silence. "Your flute playing has come a long way this week, Madison. It's amazing how playing a couple times every day speeds up your progress."

Madison nodded. She hated the long silences, but this statement didn't require an answer. She racked her brain for something to say. Nothing came to her. She could remember how it was back in Calgary. She had lots of friends. She always had something to say, someone to say it to. But her parents' divorce seemed to have affected her brain. It was constantly blank now.

Numb. The move to the coast had ended her carefree days with girls she'd known since pre-school. Friends were something she took for granted before, and now she didn't even know how to make small talk.

"Listen, Madison," said Lisa. "I can see you're not having such a great time at Band Camp. Thirteen is a tough age. Hard to break into groups. I know. I remember well. I've got to run up to the hall now, and set up for practice, but I want you to come and talk to me anytime you want. I'm here for you. Okay?"

"Okay." Madison nodded her head but didn't look up. Tears had suddenly filled her eyes and were threatening to spill down her face.

"See you in a bit then." Lisa squeezed Madison's shoulder and with a last look at her headed up the hill. Madison wiped her eyes. Lisa's kind words made her feel worse than ever. She didn't want Lisa's pity. She just wanted to be liked. And noticed. Mostly noticed.

# Chapter Two

∞ ⊙ ◇

After dinner, it was time for the Beans on Toast Award presentation. It was becoming an evening tradition, inspired by a group of senior boys. They had been on a forest hike on the first day of Band Camp and had stumbled upon a wooden plaque with the words *Beans on Toast* engraved on it. Ed, the camp director, thought that it may have been an old menu sign from when the area was the site of a logging camp. On the same hike, Graham had been showing off, lost his footing and tumbled down a steep embankment. Ed had to return to camp to get some rope to rescue him. The rest of the hikers found this hilariously funny and wanted to share the experience with their fellow band members. That evening they presented Graham with the plaque, the first ever Beans on Toast Award. They decided that every evening the person who did the most outrageous thing during the day would receive the award. The original hiking team would be the judges, and anyone could nominate a fellow camper as the winner.

Each day, campers were purposely doing outlandish things so they could be nominated for the award. Madison noticed how competitive it was becoming. The presentation was the highlight of the day. Campers called out their nominations.

"I nominate Craig for organizing last night's midnight kitchen raid."

"I nominate Kristal for capsizing her canoe during her canoe lesson."

"I nominate Brad for eating twenty-three pancakes for breakfast."

As usual, Madison sat alone watching the presentation, desperately wishing to be a part of it. Luke was one of the hikers who had discovered the plaque, so he was now a judge. As she watched him present the award to the day's winner she fantasized that she was receiving the plaque. Luke would present it to her and their eyes would meet. Luke would wonder why he hadn't noticed her before and would seek her out later that evening …

"Okay, campers," said Ed, wrapping up the award ceremony. "Remember that a week tomorrow is Talent night. Each cabin is to prepare a skit. Tonight everyone is to spend time practicing before we light the campfire. Away you go."

Madison sat on her bed, listening to the conversation.

"It's about time one of us won the Beans on Toast Award," whined Marisa. "It's not fair that it's always the older kids who win."

"Got any suggestions?" asked Ashley.

"No, but one of us must be able to do something out of the ordinary," Marisa continued.

"How about we nominate Danica for wearing the shortest skirts at camp?" suggested Alicia.

"Jealousy gets you nowhere," responded

Danica. She did a little twirl around the room so everyone could admire her long, shapely dancer's legs. "If you've got it, flaunt it, I've always said."

"So we've noticed," replied Alicia.

"We could nominate Sarah for snoring the loudest," suggested Jennifer.

"Do not!" responded Sarah.

"Do so!" replied six other girls in unison. Even Madison found herself laughing. She bet the whole camp could hear Sarah snoring.

"Let's get on with the skit," said Sarah, eager to change the subject. "We've decided on the bubblegum one, right?"

Madison listened as the girls discussed the skit. It was a good idea and she knew it would work. She looked around the room. It wasn't that she didn't like these girls. She did. Of the seven, she thought she probably liked Ashley the best. Ashley reminded her a little of Kate back in Calgary. They were both down-to-earth and funny. They were each honest, so you always knew where you stood. They even looked alike: straight, black hair cut bluntly at the shoulder; expressive, dark eyes; lashes lightly accentuated with mascara. Madison wished she was allowed to use mascara. Not till she's sixteen, said her mother. Sixteen. The magic age. The age when everything was allowed to happen: make-up, pierced ears, dating, driver's license.

Madison suddenly felt everyone looking at her. Daydreaming, she didn't know what they had asked her, what they were waiting for her to say. She felt her cheeks flush. She immediately hated her skin for this dead giveaway.

"What part would you like, Madison?" asked Marisa again.

"I don't care. Just give me any part," replied Madison. It was a lie. She did care. She would have loved to play the lead role, the girl who chewed the bubblegum, but there was no way they would give it to her anyway.

"Okay," said Marisa. "Is the old lady with the cane okay?"

"Sure."

"You'll have to do something about your hair, then," said Danica. "Old ladies don't usually have long, curly hairstyles."

"I'll stick it in a bun."

"Good. It's all decided." Marisa had taken on the role of leader tonight. "Now all we have to do is practice a few times. Jennifer, you go outside the door and the rest of us will sit around like we're in a waiting room."

The rehearsal began. Madison did as she was told, not making any suggestions or adding anything extra to her part. She felt good just being a part of the group and being included, even if they had to include her. She was sorry when 9:00 came. Campfire time.

"Aren't you coming, Madison?" asked Ashley as the group raced out the door and down to the beach.

Madison was startled. She hadn't expected anyone to notice that she was staying back this time. After the warm feeling of belonging she'd experienced while rehearsing the skit, she couldn't bear the feeling of emptiness that would come if she sat alone at the campfire— an outsider looking in.

"No, I want to finish my book tonight."

"Suit yourself," replied Ashley as she headed out after the others.

Darn, thought Madison. Ashley had made an attempt at friendship and she'd turned her down. She tried to figure out what her problem was. Maybe her mother was right. Maybe it was her own fault she didn't have any friends.

Madison studied herself in the cabin mirror. There was nothing wrong with the way she looked. Nothing wrong, but nothing great either. Her large eyes stared back at her from the mirror. They were not blue or gray. Somewhere in-between. A little mascara would help highlight her long, thick lashes. Her curly hair was her best feature and she wore it long and loose. She knew a lot of girls permed their hair to get this effect. If only Luke would notice it, she thought. She looked down at her body. She knew her breasts were finally beginning to develop. They certainly hurt when she ran, but there was nothing substantial yet. Her mom had been a late bloomer, so Madison figured she would be, too.

Madison took out her flute and sat on the front step of the cabin. No one would hear her over the noise of the campfire so she was free to pour her heart out in her music—a slow, melodic tune that matched her feelings. She began to play. Sad, aching music floated across the camp, music that she had reached down and pulled from her very soul. The sky was still streaked pink from the now-set sun and the night creatures were just beginning to rustle and creak in the forest behind her. Madison felt at peace. Just her and her music, the forest and the sunset. No one to notice she was alone.

*Bang!* The door to the washroom next door swung shut. Startled, Madison looked over at the next building. Luke stood there, staring at her. Immediately she felt her cheeks begin to burn. Of all the people to find her here, sitting alone at dusk.

Luke had to walk past her to get to the beach trail. Madison looked down, too embarrassed to meet his gaze. She heard his long stride heading past her cabin. The footsteps stopped. She had no choice but to look up. It was the first time she had ever really looked at him, she realized, not wanting to get caught staring before this. His eyes were every bit as blue as she had imagined. His blond hair was wind-tousled and hanging low over his forehead. Madison expected to see ridicule in his eyes, so she was surprised to find a look of interest—he was really studying her. Trying to decide if she'd lost her mind, she thought.

"What was the name of that song you were just playing?" he asked.

"No name. I made it up."

"Really? Wow. You've got some talent."

And that was it. He turned and left, heading down to the beach to join his friends, the laughter and the singing. He hadn't asked why she was here alone, playing her flute. Probably didn't care, Madison thought. She watched his back disappear into the darkness. She tried to get a grip on her feelings; her heart was pounding erratically. He'd actually talked to her. Said she was talented. That was more words exchanged than they'd ever had before. It was a start. Maybe tomorrow he'd say hi to her when they passed in the camp area. Maybe he'd listen for her flute when they had band practice. She was elated. He had noticed her and her music. And he liked it and cared enough to comment on it.

Madison was lying on her bed reading when the other girls returned from the campfire at 10:30. Listening to their whispers and giggles, she began to drift off. She wished Kate was here. She could tell Kate all about what had happened this evening. Kate would understand. More importantly, Kate would care.

# Chapter Three

Lisa tapped her conductor's baton on the music stand. The sound of the musicians warming up slowly died away.

"Madison, I would like to see you right after practice today." Madison nodded. "Okay, woodwinds, let's take it from the top."

It was the morning woodwind practice. Madison wondered what Lisa wanted. Probably another pep talk on being thirteen, she figured. After practice, she cleaned her flute and returned it to its case. In ten minutes the brass section of the band would be coming in. Madison thought that if her talk with Lisa lasted long enough, she might get a chance to see Luke coming in for his trumpet practice.

"Thanks for staying, Madison. I've been listening to you for the last couple of mornings, and I'm really impressed by your progress!" Lisa was wearing a big smile.

"Thanks," replied Madison. She wished Lisa would have dished out her compliments during practice so the other musicians would hear that she could do something worth noticing.

"That's why I'm thinking of assigning you to First Chair," said Lisa. "Would you like that?"

"First Chair?"

"Yeah. First Chair."

"What about Jennifer? She's First Chair."

"Not anymore, Madison. Not if you want the position. Jennifer hasn't shown any motivation to keep it, and you have come a long way this year."

Of course Madison wanted the position. It was an honor. She would get the odd solo and, more importantly, she would get noticed.

On the other hand, Madison knew Jennifer would be very unhappy about being bumped from the position. All of her friends would come to her defense, and that would not help Madison win any popularity contests. Jennifer was her cabin mate, and if she wanted to hang on to that sense of belonging that she had felt during last night's skit rehearsal, she had better not take the position.

"Are you worried about Jennifer's reaction?" asked Lisa, quietly.

"Yeah, kind of."

"It's a tough one. Only you can decide what's more important to you. Take some time—give it some thought and let me know when you've decided—one way or the other."

Madison walked out the door of the hall in a daze. She was halfway back to the cabin when she realized she hadn't even watched for Luke to come in for his practice.

Ashley was pulling on a pair of shorts when Madison entered their cabin. Kyla, Jennifer's best friend, was the only other girl in the room.

"Hi, Madison. What did Lisa want?" asked Ashley.

Madison paused before she answered. She

was pleased Ashley was interested, but she knew she had to be cautious. She glanced at Kyla, but Kyla seemed absorbed in a hand-held electronic game she was playing.

"She just wanted to tell me that I was improving."

"That's it?" asked Ashley. Madison felt Kyla staring at her now, waiting for her answer.

"Yeah." She saw the look that passed between Ashley and Kyla.

"So what are you guys doing this morning?" asked Ashley. Madison tried to mask her relief as Ashley changed the subject.

"I'm going to do crafts," answered Kyla. "They're painting T-shirts today."

"I haven't decided yet," said Madison. She took a deep breath. "How about you, Ashley?"

"I signed up for kayak lessons." She glanced at her watch. "Gotta go. See you later."

Madison wandered over to the hall, still undecided about how to fill the morning. She thought about her conversation with Ashley. Ashley had actually asked her what she was doing this morning. That was two friendly gestures in just over twelve hours …

Madison listened to the brass section practicing. Luke was part of the music she could hear coming from inside. He was First Trumpet. What should she tell Lisa about the First Flute position? Why did she even care what Jennifer thought? And what Lisa said was true; Jennifer really wasn't focusing on her music here at camp. Her mind must be on something else, Madison thought.

Picking up a ball, Madison began shooting baskets. Bounce, bounce, bounce, shoot. Her thoughts continued. If she *did* take the position, Ashley would defend Jennifer. That chance of a friendship would be ruined. After all, Ashley and Jennifer had been friends a long time and Ashley would more than likely be loyal.

Madison watched as her ball arched in the air. Just before it dropped in the hoop it was knocked off course by another basketball. Madison glanced behind her and saw that it was Ricky who had thrown the ball. Ricky played the bassoon, went to the same school and was in the same class as Madison.

"What are you doing?" asked Madison, coolly.

"Shooting baskets," he answered, grinning. "What are *you* doing?"

"I'm just waiting for the hike to start," she said, surprising herself.

"Maybe I'll go on the hike, too," he said, a little too eagerly. Madison found his enthusiasm annoying. There was nothing really wrong with Ricky. He just wasn't tall, older and blond—he wasn't Luke.

When Ed sounded the whistle a short time later to gather the hikers together, Madison had no choice but to join in, now that she had told Ricky she was going. Ricky fell into step beside her, offering to return the ball for her.

"No thanks," she said, and took a long shot at the ball bin. To her surprise the ball sailed right in.

"How about that. Flute Girl is also a basketball hot shot."

Madison looked up to find the source of the voice. It was Luke, coming out of the hall from his practice. His trumpet case swung lightly in his hand as he came down the ramp from the hall door. He was surrounded by the other brass players, who had all witnessed her long shot.

"You should hear Flute Girl play," he remarked

to no one in particular. "She really knows how to make that tin pipe sing."

"Are you guys hiking?" Ed asked the group coming down the ramp.

"Yeah, yeah," replied Luke. "We just have to put our instruments away. We'll be right back."

Madison swallowed hard. He had noticed her, talked about her and now he was also going on the hike.

"Why did he call you 'Flute Girl'?" asked Ricky.

"It's a long story," lied Madison. She hoped Ricky wasn't going to be a pest on this hike. She really wanted a chance to watch Luke and his friends, hoping Luke would notice her again.

# Chapter Four

The air felt cool and moist under the mix of fir, cedar and coastal pine trees as the hikers followed Ed onto the forest trail. It was a relief to get away from the glare of the sun and the mid-morning heat.

"Let's take the upper trail today," suggested Ed, "so we can get a view of the islands from the cliff." Ed led the way, and the hikers, in small groups, followed behind. Ricky stayed right with Madison, working hard to keep pace with her long strides. Madison, in turn, was trying to keep up with the older boys, who were listening to

Ed rattle off facts about the various plants and bushes they passed along the way.

"Fresh deer droppings," he announced, squatting over a small pile on the side of the trail. "Can't be more than an hour old."

"What other animals are in this forest?" asked Ricky.

"Bear, raccoon, skunk, opossum," he listed. "We're not likely to see many, though, we're making too much noise. And most animals have a keen sense of smell. They'll be long gone before we can get anywhere near them."

"Did you say bears?" asked Ricky.

"Yeah. But don't worry. They'll want to avoid you just as much as you want to avoid them. But we can watch for their tracks and droppings. That way we'll know if they're in the vicinity."

Ed was now leading the group up a steep hill. Through the trees, Madison caught the odd glimpse of the ocean far below them. The wind had picked up and there were whitecaps on the water.

"You'll notice how noisy the birds are right now," Ed commented. "By noon, it will grow quite quiet in the woods. The birds seem to take a siesta during the hottest part of the day."

Madison felt invigorated from the climb. She had quit trying to keep up with the older boys and was actually enjoying Ricky's company. She could be herself with him. And he must like her— it was his idea to tag along. She liked the way her leg muscles ached as they climbed up the winding trail. It had been awhile since she had exercised and it felt good.

A blood-curdling scream suddenly shattered the morning tranquility. It came from the forest, somewhere to their right. The hikers came to an abrupt halt and all eyes turned to Ed for an explanation. But Ed looked as shocked as the campers did. They listened for a moment. The forest was still; even the noisy birds had grown quiet. Then a cat-like growl broke the silence. It sounded very close.

"Strange," whispered Ed. "Sounds like a warning."

"Then let's turn around and go back," whispered Ricky. There was a general nod of agreement among the hikers. Madison felt her heart pounding in her chest. She turned with the others, anxious to get out of the woods, the sooner the better.

"Hang on, guys. Not so fast. I think we should

find out what it is," suggested Ed quietly. "Otherwise our imaginations might work overtime tonight." He considered the situation a moment longer. "Let's take a peek in the forest. We'll be okay if we stick together."

The hikers looked skeptical, but no one argued with Ed. After all, he was the experienced outdoorsman. They followed him as he picked his way through the dense trees. Madison glanced at Luke. She noticed the usual cool, self-assured expression had left his face and he looked just as scared as the rest of them.

Not far from the trail, Ed stopped abruptly. The campers quickly caught up with him and there were gasps of shock as they each noticed what had made him pause. A large, golden animal lay sprawled on the forest floor; its lifeless eyes staring blankly at the group. Madison was aware of a nauseating smell coming from the animal. She covered her nose with the crook of her arm and took a step backward.

"It's a dead cougar," said Ed. He studied the large cat quietly. "It must have somehow been injured. Look at its hind leg. It's a mangled mess."

"What do you think happened to it?" Luke asked.

"Well, maybe it got gored by a buck's antler," Ed said. "Or maybe it's a gunshot wound— though I sure hope not. It's hard to say, though. Poor animal must have died of an infection, judging by the smell."

"If it's dead, what made the noise?" asked Ricky.

The hikers were quiet, contemplating the question. Suddenly Madison had the strange feeling that she was being watched. She looked up into the majestic trees around them. The sunlight was filtering down through the treetops, casting the forest in dappled shade. It was hard to make out shapes, but Madison thought she saw two sets of golden eyes staring down at the crowd from high up in a nearby tree.

"Look, there's something up there," she whispered, pointing in the direction of the eyes.

Just then, a hiss came from the tree. Then a growl.

"More cougars," whispered Ed. "Stay still."

As Madison peered into the tree, she began to make out the shape of the bodies behind the black-rimmed eyes. Sure enough, there were two cats perched in the branches. One of them suddenly snarled and clawed at the air, as if warning the group to stay back. As scared as she felt

herself, Madison sensed the animal was even more terrified.

"They must be the kittens of this cougar," whispered Ed, indicating the dead cat in front of them. "That would explain why they're here. Cougars live alone, except for kittens with their mother."

"They don't look like kittens," whispered Luke. Madison could hear a tremble in his voice.

"They're probably about a year old. Cougar young stay with their mother for up to a year and a half."

"What are we going to do?" whispered Ricky.

"We're going to stay together and slowly back out onto the trail. Keep facing the cats. When they see us retreating they'll probably relax. Let's go."

When the group reached the trail they began to jog back to camp. Madison couldn't help but glance back a couple of times, wondering if they were being followed. They arrived a few minutes later, breathless and excited. Ed went straight to his radiophone to contact a conservation officer.

♪ ♪ ♪

Word of the incident traveled fast and by lunch the entire group knew about the cougar. After lunch, Ed called a meeting of all the campers, counselors and staff.

"As you've no doubt heard," he began, " this morning's hiking group came upon a dead cougar. We also saw two other cougars in a tree. As I explained earlier, these wildcats tend to live alone in a territory they have carefully staked out. The territories are usually quite large so that the cougar can find enough food. The only exception to this is when a female has a litter. The kittens stay with their mother for eighteen months or more.

"I talked to a conservation officer when we got back this morning and told him about the dead cougar and her kittens. He said we should just leave the dead cougar alone, that nature would take its course."

"What about the kittens?" Danica asked. "Do you think they're dangerous?"

"Well, from what I understand, there're only three reasons a cougar would attack a person: if it was starving, sick or injured, or provoked. Judging by the size of them, these two juveniles are probably about a year old. There's a good chance they'll make a go of it on their own, but there's no doubt that they're scared and confused right now and probably still honing their hunting skills. For those reasons they might pose a slight danger, so it is especially important that campers only enter the woods with a hiking group, led by me. People disobeying these rules could be putting themselves in danger and will be sent home, no questions asked. Am I quite clear?"

The campers nodded and grew quiet, feeling bad for the dead mother cougar and for the cougar kittens—now motherless.

The hall was unusually quiet during dinner that night. When it was time for the Beans on Toast Award, the judges huddled together, looking very serious. There had been a few half-hearted nominations, but the usual enthusiasm was missing.

"We've made a decision," announced Justin after consulting the other judges. "The Beans on Toast Award will not be presented to a camper today. The award presentation will resume tomorrow night.

"Instead, we would like to honor the dead cougar and its kittens tonight." One of the other judges produced a candle and Luke struck a match. As Luke lit the candle, Justin continued, "We light this candle in memory of the mother cougar and in hope that the kittens can make it on their own." Then he added, "Let's have a moment of silence."

Madison felt a lump in her throat. She blinked hard, noticing a few sniffles coming from around her. She respected the decision the boys had made and was amazed that none of the other campers were scornful of the ceremony. Ed finally broke the silence.

"Campfire will be at 9:00, as usual. You can decide for yourselves whether you will practice your skits tonight."

The campers milled around the common area, talking in small groups. Madison realized they felt a need to be together, much like after a funeral service. No one seemed anxious to practice their skits. She sat on the hall steps, Ricky quietly sitting beside her. She glanced at him. His short, dark hair was carefully parted and combed neatly into place. His baggy T-shirt and cutoffs looked clean and pressed. A gold hoop in one ear sparkled as it caught the evening light. He *was* pleasant-looking. So why didn't she feel more attracted to him? Maybe if he was taller, she thought, she wouldn't feel so awkward around him.

The song she often played was singing in her head. She wished she could get out her flute and play, releasing the emotions she felt—sorrow for the dead cougar and worry for her kittens. But today would end on a note of hope. She actually felt a part of this quiet group. Sad as it had turned out, she had been on the hike when the cougar was found. Ashley had been acting friendly, Ricky obviously liked her and Luke had noticed her again. No, she couldn't get out her flute right now with all these people around, but she knew she could face the campfire tonight with Ricky there to sit with. And tomorrow didn't look quite so threatening. Hey, maybe she'd even find a way to win the Beans on Toast Award and get everyone to notice her before the end of camp. Maybe.

# Chapter Five

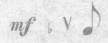

Sunday was visiting day at Band Camp. Family and friends were invited to come and spend the day with the campers and then listen to an informal band concert in the afternoon. The first water taxi was expected at 11:00 a.m., delivering the guests to the coastal camp.

Madison looked forward to seeing her mother, but dreaded the inevitable questions: Are you having fun? Have you made lots of friends? What have you been doing? She practiced the answers in her head as she watched the cove, expecting to see the first boat at any minute.

*"Are you having fun?"*

"No, I'm having a lousy time and I want to go home," … or … "It's all right. I guess I can hang in there for another week." Madison decided on the second choice. She'd look like a cry-baby leaving halfway through the two-week camp.

*"Have you made lots of friends?"*

How could she say, "Well, I made one friend just yesterday, and Ashley is beginning to act friendly … maybe by the end of camp I might have a girlfriend. And then there's Luke. He noticed me. Does that make him a friend?" Madison knew her mom would be disappointed. She so badly wanted Madison to be happy. And Madison had tried … hadn't she? No, she'd have to tell her mom a white lie about the friends … hopefully her mom wouldn't notice.

*"What have you been doing?"*

"Well, aside from music practices, I've pretty much just been reading, or hanging about. Yesterday I actually found myself on a hike and we came across a dead cougar and her two orphaned kittens." Oh, yeah. Her mom would really like hearing about that.

Madison quit rehearsing answers when she saw the small boat coming around the point. She studied the faces in the boat, looking for her mother. Sure enough, there she was, right at the front, her worried face scanning the beach for her daughter. Madison waved and strolled down to the pier. A few other campers were headed down to the dock, too, being careful not to look *too* excited about seeing their parents. For a moment Madison thought that she saw her father, sitting tall and proud beside her mother, but then realized that it was someone else. She knew in her heart that her father wasn't coming, but she couldn't help wishing things were different—that he could be here. They would shoot some baskets together, play tennis and maybe even go for a swim. But her mother was here alone, just like Madison knew she would be. And her mother would want to talk—would want to know all about camp life.

"Hi, Madison! You look great! So tanned!"

"Hi, Mom." Madison pulled herself away from her mother's tight embrace. "How are you?"

"Oh, the same, you know. Lonely for you, but not much else to report."

Madison showed her mom around the campsite. She felt conspicuous, being just the two of them. Most of the others were in large family groups with brothers and sisters. Many of the families knew each other and were talking and laughing loudly together as they reminisced about Band Camp in years gone by and caught up on each other's lives.

After the tour of the camp, Madison and her mom sat on a bench outside the hall and watched the other families socialize. Her mom hadn't asked any of the anticipated questions. This was driving Madison crazy. What was the problem? Did she think Madison was unlikable, unable to make friends?

Madison made a point of joining Ricky and his family at lunch. Many of the families were taking their food outside for a picnic, so there was lots of room at Ricky's table.

"Can we sit with you, Ricky?" Madison asked, noticing that both Ricky's parents and sister were there for the visit.

"Sure, shove over, Annie," he said to his little sister.

Ricky's family looked nice, thought Madison. Uncomplicated. Unsophisticated. She was relieved to have someone to join so her mother wouldn't know she often ate alone.

"I was just telling my parents about the hike we were on when we found the cougar," Ricky told Madison. Her mom looked at her, astonished. Ricky noticed. "Didn't you tell your mom about it yet, Madison?" He directed his story to her mom. "Yeah, yesterday Madison and I were on a hike and we came across a cougar, just off the trail."

"Just you and Madison?"

"No, Mom. We were with a whole group, and Ed, the camp director," said Madison, annoyed that her mother missed the point of the story. She knew her mother would find something to worry about, but she thought it would be the cougar, not the possibility of her being alone with a boy.

"The cougar was dead but her two kittens were up a tree, hissing and growling at us." Ricky was enjoying the chance to tell the story twice. "They're about a year old, so they don't look like kittens. In fact, they're pretty darn big. It's really sad, though, because now the kittens are on their own."

"Hmm," said Madison's mom when Ricky finished the story. An awkward silence followed. No one seemed to know what to say next.

Madison noticed Lisa come into the hall for a second helping of lunch. She spotted Madison and her mother sitting with Ricky's family and came over to their table.

"Welcome to Band Camp, Mrs. Turner," Lisa said, reaching out to shake her hand. "I'm really pleased with Madison's progress this week," she continued as she sat down across the table. Then she turned to Madison. "Did you tell your mom about the promotion I offered you?"

Madison felt her face flush. Without actually looking at Ricky, she felt his startled reaction. He would be all ears, waiting for her answer.

"No. I haven't made a decision," answered Madison. She looked hard at Lisa, hoping she'd drop the subject, fast.

Lisa looked around the table, realized her blunder and then tried to get Madison off the hook, but without much success. "Madison is qualified to take First Chair, but she hasn't decided whether or not she's ready for the responsibility." She looked back at Madison with an apologetic expression on her face.

"Of course she's ready," answered her mother. "That's wonderful, dear."

"What's there to decide?" asked Ricky. "That's an honor anyone would accept." He looked confused, searching Madison's face for an explanation.

"Everyone except me," replied Madison. "Let's drop the subject."

Another awkward silence descended on the table. Madison felt mortified. Now her mother would be on her back about taking First Chair, and Ricky would be blabbing the news to the others before she could make her own decision.

"I'd better go say hi to a few more parents," said Lisa, getting up. She looked around the table. Madison refused to make eye contact with her. "I'll see you all at the concert this afternoon."

Ricky's family began picking up their plates, getting ready to leave.

"It was nice meeting you and your mom, Madison," said Ricky's dad. His mom smiled at them as they turned to leave.

"See you later," said Mrs. Turner.

Madison scrambled to her feet and caught up with Ricky before he reached the kitchen.

She grabbed his arm and whispered in his ear.

"Don't breathe a word to anyone about what Lisa said."

"Why not?" He studied her face. "You should be proud of yourself."

"Just don't," she said, glaring at him. He shrugged his shoulders as Madison returned to her mother.

"What's going on now, Madi?" Madison noticed the emphasis on the word "now" as if she was always doing something wrong.

"Nothing is going on *now*, Mom. I just don't know if I want the position."

"I don't understand you, Madison," sighed her mother. "You've worked so hard at your music, and now you turn down the opportunity to play First Flute."

"I haven't turned it down, Mom. I just haven't decided yet." Madison thought about explaining the situation to her, but that would mean confessing that she hadn't made any friends yet, and that would disappoint her mom even more. No, it was better that her mom thought she had made friends and just didn't want the responsibility of First Chair. Her mom wouldn't understand how her cabin mates, even Ashley, would have to come to Jennifer's defense, the current First Chair.

The bass drum boomed, announcing the start of the "Family Feud Volleyball Competition." Madison and her mom headed out to the field where Ed sorted the families into fairly even-sized teams.

"The Turner family," he said, addressing Madison and her mom, "The Turners are with the Gills and Mathisons. You're up first."

As she played, Madison was aware of Ricky watching her from the sidelines, where he awaited his turn in the round-robin competition. She was also aware of Luke on the other side of the net, playing with his family. They had been teamed up with Jennifer's. As Jennifer got prepared to serve the ball, Madison heard Luke's smooth voice cheering her on.

"C'mon, Jennifer, you can do it. Sock it to them!" Jennifer served the ball and it sailed over the net right to Madison's mom, who should have been able to return it easily. But she gave a little scream and ducked, and the ball landed

behind her while the rest of the team looked
on.

"I'm sorry. I'm sorry. I wasn't ready for that.
I'll get it next time. Don't worry." Madison just
hoped there wouldn't be a next time.

"Come on, Jenny. Do it again!" Luke was
cheering Jennifer on again. *Whack.* Jennifer hit
the ball and it headed straight for Madison's
mom again. Madison could see her begin to
duck, so she quickly came to the rescue. She
flew across the court, bumping the ball high
enough for her mom to volley it across. This
time her mom made contact with the ball, but
not hard enough to send it back across the net.

"Darn!" said her mom, examining her hand.
"Broke a nail."

Jennifer prepared to serve again. As the ball
sailed toward the backcourt, Madison could
hear Luke congratulating Jennifer on another
great serve. This time the ball flew past Madison's mom and was successfully volleyed to the
front row where Madison waited. Fueled by anger and jealousy, she leapt up to the sagging
net and spiked the ball down hard. The other
team didn't have a chance. Madison had regained control of the game for her team. She

could hear Ricky cheering for her from the sidelines. She didn't dare look at Luke.

But Madison's sense of victory didn't last long. The next serve was volleyed back and forth. Her teammates were covering for her mom and the crowd was cheering. Then the ball was at the net, on Luke's side. His brother, just as tall and athletic as Luke, jumped up to spike the ball. Madison's mom had somehow become turned around, and the ball came down hard on the back of her head. Madison watched in horror as her mom crumpled into an unconscious heap in the grass.

# Chapter Six

Madison's mother quickly regained consciousness as Ed squatted over her, checking her vital signs. For a moment, Madison thought she was dead. The disturbing sight of her mom's inert form was so similar to the dead cougar's that she wondered, afterwards, if she had howled in distress, just as the cougar kitten had. Mrs. Turner tried to stand up and carry on as if nothing had happened, but Ed insisted on escorting her to the medical cabin where she could rest.

Madison's anguish suddenly turned to shame. She felt everyone's eyes on her as she left the volleyball court with Ed and her mother. Her face was burning and she kept her eyes glued to the ground in front of her. This was not how she planned to get noticed. Her mother looked like a fool and now Madison was going to have to live it down.

Madison stayed with her mother while she rested. After about an hour she insisted she was fine, so they decided to return to the tournament as spectators. To Madison's surprise, the game came to a halt when the crowd spotted them approaching the volleyball court. Everyone stood and cheered for her mother, looking regal and composed as she crossed the field, chin held high. Someone fetched a lawnchair that she accepted gracefully. Luke's brother made his way through the crowd to speak to her.

"I'm really sorry about the spike, Mrs. Turner," he apologized. "It was an accident. I didn't mean to hurt anyone."

"I know," she answered. "I was in the wrong place at the wrong time. Evidently I was facing the wrong way, too. I should have learned to stay out of sports years ago." She smiled warmly. Madison was surprised at her mother's grace. If it had happened to her, she would have been mortified. She felt uneasy, thinking about how angry her mother's accident had made her just an hour ago. Now here she was, admiring her mom's poise and good humor. She was ashamed at how selfish her reaction had been.

The concert went well, and Madison's mom left with the other visitors. She didn't ask any more questions about the First Chair situation or about Madison's lack of friends. Madison hugged her mom tightly before she boarded the boat.

"Hang in there, kiddo," were her mother's parting words. Madison was startled. Maybe she *does* understand more than I give her credit for, she thought.

Ricky sat with her during dinner. As far as she could tell, he hadn't told anyone about her possible promotion to First Chair.

"It's time for the Beans on Toast Award," announced Andrew to the crowd. An expectant silence descended over the hall. "Today's winner is unusual in that he is actually a graduate of the band. In fact, he's not even here tonight. But his little brother, 'Lukey,' has offered to accept the award in his place."

Madison felt her face flush. She could see where this was going and she couldn't believe the boys saw any humor in it. Frozen to her seat, she didn't want to stay any longer, yet she couldn't make her feet move.

Andrew carried on. "Today's winner is Spike, also known as Matthew Lewis, for his incredible skill, precision and force in literally clobbering the other team." The hall came alive with cheering and clapping. Luke accepted the award for his brother, held it over his head and bowed to the crowd. As they rose in a standing ovation, Madison finally found her feet and raced out of the hall. Ricky followed close behind.

Once outside, Madison didn't know where to run. Going to the cabin was pointless because the others would be there shortly. There was nowhere to go where she could be completely alone. Nowhere, that was, except the forest. Ricky caught up with her just as she headed into the trees.

"You'll get sent home for going in there."

"Good. I'd like to go home. Get away from these morons."

"C'mon, Madison. They didn't mean anything by it. It had nothing to do with your mother. It could have been anyone. They were just finding the humor in the situation."

"I don't think so."

"Well I know so." Ricky grabbed Madison's arm as she moved deeper into the forest and held her still. "You're too sensitive. That's your biggest problem. You could have laughed along with them—no big deal."

"My mother could have been seriously hurt."

"But she wasn't. They wouldn't have joked about it if she'd really been hurt."

"I'm not so sure about that." But she found herself beginning to calm down. She shook herself loose from Ricky's grip and plunked down on a large, flat rock. Ricky sat beside her. Madison could see the campground through the trees, but she knew they'd be hidden in the shadows of the large cedars.

"So you think I'm too sensitive, eh?"

"Yeah. A little."

"Why do you think that?" she asked. The anger was gone now, but she wasn't ready to face the others yet.

"You're probably afraid to take First Chair because of what Jennifer will say. I say, who cares? She didn't do the job—she doesn't get the recognition."

"Boys are different that way."

"Yeah? How?"

"All the others will defend Jennifer because she's one of them. I'll never make any friends." Madison knew she was whining, but she couldn't help herself.

"Who wants to be friends with them if they act that way?" Ricky turned to look at her. She noticed how nice his eyes were. He actually looked like he cared. It was a long time before Madison answered.

"I do. I really need some friends."

Madison felt Ricky's arm drape around her shoulder. "I'm your friend. Why don't you tell Jennifer, privately, what Lisa offered you and see what happens? I'll still be your friend."

Ricky's arm around her shoulder was making Madison uncomfortable. She wasn't sure if it was really just a friendly gesture or the start of something more. She didn't wait to find out. She jumped up, knocking him over in the process.

"We better go back," she said.

"Are you going to tell her?" he asked, picking himself up and brushing off his shorts. "She has a right to know."

"I don't know."

Madison and Ricky managed to leave the forest unnoticed. Madison realized that Ricky had taken a big chance following her into the trees. True, they hadn't gone very far, but he had been willing to take the risk for her.

When she got back to the cabin, the girls were busy practicing their skit.

"Where have you been, Madison?" asked Danica.

"Off with Ricky, her new boyfriend, I bet," said Sarah before Madison had a chance to respond. That got everyone's attention.

"Ricky Nylon?" asked Danica. "Nerd Nylon?"

Madison could feel everyone's eyes on her, waiting for an answer. She glanced at Ashley. Ashley was looking at the floor, not willing to meet Madison's eyes. Madison could feel her heart pounding, partly in anger and partly in embarrassment. She felt like turning around and leaving, but she didn't want to give Danica the satisfaction. She forced herself to remain calm.

"None of your business, Danica," she answered, hoping to sound more confident than she felt. "Sorry I'm late," she continued. "Where are you in the practice?"

There was a long silence in the cabin. The girls were waiting for Danica to react. Madison met her gaze, wondering what it was she saw in her eyes. Anger? Scorn? Maybe a hint of respect for standing her ground?

"Let's take it from the beginning." Ashley came to the rescue. "Jennifer," she said, "step outside and the rest of us will take our places. C'mon, guys, let's get on with it."

This time Ashley's eyes did meet Madison's. Ashley was smiling. Madison smiled back and hoped Ashley would sense her gratitude.

Madison joined the others on the beach for the evening campfire. Sitting alone on a log facing the flames was Ricky. He motioned for her to join him, but Madison ignored the invitation and sat with the girls from her cabin. When she glanced back at him, he was still watching her, looking puzzled and disappointed.

Later that night, as Madison tossed and turned in bed, rehashing the events of the day, she regretted her snub. Ricky had been there for her when she needed him. She knew her reaction was a result of Danica's cruel words, and she wished she'd had the guts to ignore her and sit with Ricky. But there was something else bothering her, too. Ricky had put his arm around her tonight, supposedly in friendship. Madison had pushed him away. She sensed there was more to his gesture. Perhaps he liked her—more than as just a friend.

Madison flipped over in bed one last time. What a long, confusing day it had been. She wondered sleepily what tomorrow would bring.

# Chapter Seven

Madison successfully avoided Ricky all morning, but he finally caught up with her as she was scraping her lunch plate into the garbage.

"How are you today?" he asked cheerfully.

"Fine, I guess. How 'bout you?" She felt too awkward to make eye contact with him. She wondered if he knew she had been avoiding him.

"You were pretty angry when I talked to you last night."

"Oh, yeah. That. Well, I got over it."

"Good. So have you made a decision about First Chair?"

"As a matter of fact, I have." Madison finally looked directly at him. They were outside now, walking with no particular destination in mind. They had about ten minutes before they would have to return to their cabins for rest time. "I've decided not to accept it. Jennifer's still a good flute player, and I don't play well under pressure. I'd freeze up if I had to play a solo."

Ricky stopped walking and turned to face her. "That's bull, and you know it." Madison was surprised at the anger in his voice. "I thought you had more guts than that."

"Listen, Ricky," Madison shot back. "When I talked to Lisa this morning she said I could still take the position in the fall if I wanted it then. And besides, this whole thing is none of your business anyway."

"That's a cop-out, Madison." His voice no longer held anger, just disappointment. He turned and walked away.

"And I'd appreciate you keeping this thing to yourself," Madison called to his retreating back. He only shrugged his shoulders in response. She kicked the post of the basketball hoop as she walked past it. Of all the people in the band who wanted to be her friend, it had to be him. She had a mother to make her feel constantly guilty. She didn't need him, too.

♪ ♪ ♪

Madison banged the door shut as she entered the cabin. Everyone looked up.

"What's the matter, Madison?" asked Ashley kindly.

"Nothing, really." Madison braced herself for a snide remark from someone, but there was only silence. Madison and Ashley locked eyes for a moment before Ashley returned to the conversation that had been going on when Madison entered the cabin.

"He wants you to do what?" asked Danica, talking to Jennifer.

"Meet me here during tonight's campfire," answered Jennifer. Madison wondered who "he" was, but figured it must be Jeff, the trombone player that Jennifer had her eye on.

"But you know the rule about having boys in our cabin."

"I know. That's what I told him. But he said no one would ever notice we were missing."

Madison lay on her bed listening to the conversation. She wondered if she'd break the rules for Luke. Not that she thought she would ever get the chance.

"Are you going to do it?" asked Marisa.

"I haven't decided," answered Jennifer. "But it sure is tempting."

After the hour was up, Madison remained on her bed. She didn't have the desire to do anything. Most of the girls hurried out, heading toward the concession that was only open for fifteen minutes every afternoon. Ashley stayed behind to change into her bathing suit.

"Want to talk about it, Madison?" asked Ashley.

"Talk about what?" replied Madison, tiredly.

"You look like you just lost your best friend."

"You have to have a best friend to lose one," replied Madison, but she smiled as she said it, looked at Ashley and they both laughed. "I guess in a way I did just lose my best friend," she continued. She decided to confide in Ashley. A little, anyway. "Ricky was about the only friend I have around here and I just had a big argument with him." Madison watched Ashley for her reaction. "But Danica's wrong; he's not my boyfriend. He's just someone I can talk to."

"That's the best kind of boyfriend to have," replied Ashley.

"What do you mean?"

"Well, you don't want the kind of boyfriend who only has one thing on his mind."

"You mean … sex?" asked Madison.

"Yeah. And believe me. That's what a lot of boys are after."

"So I've heard," said Madison. "I wouldn't know. Ricky's about the only boy who has ever paid any attention to me."

"Believe me, it's no fun finding out the hard way. You think this guy really likes you and then he gets you alone and his hands are all over you. When you tell him you're not interested, not yet anyway, you never hear from him again. It's a bit hard on the old ego."

"Well at least you've had the opportunity to say no. I haven't even got that far yet." Madison felt relaxed. Ashley was easy to talk to.

"You will," answered Ashley. "And then you'll realize what a nice guy Ricky actually is."

"I know what a nice guy Ricky is," answered Madison. "But I don't find him … well, you know what I mean. Anyway, it doesn't matter. I don't think he's even my friend anymore."

"What did you do?" asked Ashley.

"It's a long story," replied Madison. She realized she had better change the subject, quickly. As much as she was enjoying sharing confidences with Ashley, she knew she wasn't ready to tell her about the First Chair situation. Not yet, anyway. "Are you going swimming?"

"No, I feel like canoeing. Want to come?"

"You'll have to teach me how. I'm from Calgary, remember?"

"No problem," laughed Ashley. "Let's get down there before all the canoes are taken."

Madison and Ashley spent most of the afternoon lying lazily in the bottom of the canoe, sunbathing and getting to know one another. Madison told Ashley all about her parents' divorce and how she hated leaving Calgary to come to the coast with her mother. Ashley was very sympathetic, even though her parents were happily married. She told Madison what it was like having three younger brothers and being expected to help constantly. Madison agreed that being an only child didn't seem so bad after hearing about Ashley's family. They didn't notice how far the canoe drifted while they were talking. Suddenly Ashley sat up.

"It's 4:15. We've only got fifteen minutes until band practice."

Madison picked up her paddle as she looked around. "We've drifted a long way. You better show me what to do again."

Madison began to giggle, she felt so awkward. Behind her, Ashley was paddling with all her might, but watching Madison struggle with her paddle made her laugh, too. Another ten minutes went by before they could pull themselves together enough to paddle again. They were going against the current, so by the time they arrived at the dock, the beach area was deserted. It was almost 5:00 when they showed up for practice. They encountered Ed as they were heading up the path to the hall. When they hadn't shown up for practice at 4:30, Lisa had reported them missing. Ed was just about to put together a search team. He was fuming.

"Where were you two?"

"Canoeing. We lost track of the time," reported Ashley.

"Inexcusable! You two will report to me after dinner tonight." He stormed away. Madison looked at Ashley, wondering whether she was upset. She didn't want anything to ruin this new-found friendship. But Ashley was snickering.

"Man, was he steamed!" she said, as they continued up the hill to the hall.

"What do you think he'll do to us?" asked Madison, who was not used to getting in trouble.

"Probably whip us—fifteen lashes apiece." The two girls fell into hysterical laughter again. They could barely contain themselves as they tried to sneak, unnoticed, into band practice. Lisa stopped the music with a tap of her baton on the music stand.

"I'm glad to see you two weren't eaten by a cougar or anything," she commented. There were a few chuckles. Unlike Ed, she didn't seem too annoyed. "You know the rule for late musicians, though," she added. "You can stay behind today and clean up. And for being a whole half an hour late, you can be on set-up and take-down duty for the rest of the week."

♪ ♪ ♪

Madison felt giddy for the rest of the afternoon. She didn't care what punishment Ed gave her. It had been a long time since she'd experienced the pleasure of friendship. So when Ed tapped her on the shoulder just before the Beans on Toast Award was to be presented, she didn't mind. She'd lost interest in the award since last night, anyway. Ed took the two girls into his office.

"Do you know why I was so angry at you two this afternoon?" he asked.

"Because we were late," Ashley answered.

"It wasn't so much that you were late," he said. "It was that you were missing. We didn't know where you were and so we were concerned. Being *late* is just being rude. Being *missing* is serious. Any number of things could have happened to you. And I'm responsible for your safety." He paused, as if waiting for an answer. Madison said the only thing she could think of.

"We're sorry."

"Being sorry isn't enough, I'm afraid. There has to be a punishment. Normally I like the punishment to fit the crime, but in this case I think some simple hard work is in order. Ashley, you'll be working in the kitchen tonight with the kitchen staff. You'll help with all the cleanup, as well as all the preparation for tomorrow. You'll stay as long as the staff stays, helping in any way you can."

"Yes, sir," replied Ashley. The ladies who worked in the kitchen were a lot of fun, so Madison knew Ashley's evening wouldn't be so bad.

"And you, Madison, are to thoroughly clean all three washrooms. That means mopping the floor, cleaning the toilets and wiping down the mirrors and sinks. You'll find all the equipment you need in the cleaning supply room. Any questions?"

"No, sir," was Madison's reply. She'd had lots of experience cleaning at home. It would be lonelier work than Ashley's, but she'd had such a wonderful afternoon that it was well worth the inconvenience.

As Madison finished cleaning the third washroom, she looked at her watch. It was already 9:45. There was no point going to the campfire now. She thought she might check the kitchen after she put the cleaning supplies away to see if Ashley was still working. As she left the wash-room, now sparkling clean, she noticed a light on in her cabin. Maybe Ashley was already back in the cabin. She'd check there first.

When Madison approached the cabin she could hear giggling. Curious, she opened the door quietly. There, sitting with their backs to her, were Jennifer and Luke. Luke was leaning toward Jennifer, his hands cupping her face. Jennifer was giggling and pretending to push him away. Madison felt like the wind had just been knocked out of her. Frozen to the spot, she watched as Luke leaned forward and kissed Jennifer on the mouth. This time Jennifer didn't resist and she kissed him back. That's when Madison came to her senses. She swallowed the lump in her throat and backed up, trying to leave unnoticed.

*Crash!* The mop she was still carrying hit the doorframe and knocked the bucket over. Jennifer and Luke whirled around in panic. When they saw who it was, they visibly relaxed.

"It's just Flute Girl," said Luke, breathing a sigh of relief.

"Why are you spying on us?" yelled Jennifer. "Get a life! Get out of here!"

The shock of finding them together, combined with Luke's remark about it being "just" Flute Girl, as if she wasn't of any significance, and then being yelled at by Jennifer, was too much for Madison. She felt something snap.

"My name is Madison, for your information," she told Luke, the tension she was feeling evident in her voice. "And I wasn't spying on you. I was simply entering the cabin that happens to be mine, too!"

"Well, you can take your stupid bucket and get out of here, now!" ordered Jennifer.

"Cool it, Jennifer. Flute Girl, I mean, Madison, doesn't mean any harm. Do you, Madison?"

Madison recognized his patronizing tone of voice. He was trying to charm her. It made her sick. She knew they were worried about her squealing on them.

"If you're worried about me telling Ed about you two, I just might." Madison could feel her anger build. "And while I'm at it … I just might tell Lisa that I'm taking First Chair, too. You won't need it when you get sent home for being here."

# Chapter Eight

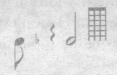

"What are you talking about?" asked Jennifer. She had moved away from Luke and was now standing in front of Madison, looking down at her. She was only a year older, but she was quite a bit taller.

But Madison couldn't be intimidated. Adrenaline was pumping through her body and she was on a roll.

"That's right! Lisa offered me First Chair."

"Why don't I know anything about this?" asked Jennifer, not sure whether to believe Madison or not.

"Because I had decided not to take the position. But I just changed my mind," she replied bitterly.

"You little … !"

"What's going on?" asked Ashley. She walked into the cabin in time to see Jennifer push Madison down on the bed.

"Your little friend here thinks she's such a hot shot!" answered Jennifer. "She claims Lisa offered her First Chair."

Ashley glanced at Luke, who was standing in a corner, squirming and looking very uncomfortable. Then she looked at Jennifer and Madison, who were glaring at each other. The situation became crystal-clear to Ashley.

"You better get out of here, Luke," she said. "It's almost 10:00. Everyone will be coming back soon. I'll talk to these two."

Luke hesitated. There was something he needed to say before he left.

"Madison, I'd really appreciate it if you kept this to yourself. You seem to have a problem with Jennifer, but I really didn't mean any harm. Can I count on you?"

Madison realized the power she suddenly held. Luke had dropped the patronizing tone and was pleading with her. He didn't want to be sent home.

"I don't know," was all she could say. She couldn't stay mad at Luke. But she wanted to punish Jennifer. Why couldn't Jennifer have fallen for someone else?

When Luke had slipped out the door, Ashley turned to Madison.

"Is it true about First Chair?"

Madison nodded.

"Why didn't you tell me? I thought we were friends." The look of disappointment on Ashley's face was almost too much for Madison to bear.

"It didn't have anything to do with us, Ashley," Madison pleaded. "I had to decide myself."

"So what are you going to do?" demanded Jennifer. "Are you going to squeal? Are you going to take First Chair?"

Madison glanced at Ashley, looking for support, but all she got was a cold stare back. The door banged open behind them. The other girls were back from the campfire. They quickly sensed the tension in the cabin.

"What's going on here?" asked Danica. "Did

someone die?"

Ashley and Jennifer continued to stare at Madison. Soon everyone was looking at her. Madison finally did what she always did when things got to be too much. She fled. Out into the cool night she ran. Across the field, past the hall toward the forest. She passed among the first trees and stopped running. What was she doing? She couldn't go into the forest at night. Too scary. But where could she go? She couldn't go back to the cabin and face all those girls, especially Ashley. She headed down the hill toward the beach, picking her way carefully in the dark. She could smell the smoke of the campfire, and then saw a small blaze at the pit on the beach. She could hear voices talking softly. She walked a little closer, trying to make out who it was. She knew she would be in trouble for being on the beach alone at night, but she didn't care. Being sent home would be a relief after tonight.

Madison recognized the silhouettes of Ed and Lisa still sitting at the fire, talking. Seeing them helped Madison come to a decision. It hadn't required any thought and came to her suddenly. She knew it was the only thing she could do. As she approached the fire, Ed spotted the figure coming toward them.

"Who's there?" he called into the night.

"It's just me, Madison Turner," she answered. She approached the fire so they could see her more clearly.

"What are you doing here, Madison?" asked Ed. "It's past curfew."

"I want to go home," she answered. "Right away."

There was silence while Ed and Lisa studied her. Then Lisa got up and walked over to Madison, putting an arm around her.

"Are you okay?" she asked softly.

The lump in her throat kept Madison from speaking. She just nodded her head. Lisa looked over Madison's head at Ed. A message passed silently between them and Ed suddenly got up.

"Make sure you two put out the fire when you're through," he said and then left, heading up the hill to the camp.

"Did something happen?" asked Lisa, gently pulling Madison down onto the log beside her.

Madison nodded. The lump in her throat threatened to choke her and she could feel the tears pour down her cheeks.

"Let it all out, Madison, and then you'll feel better."

Madison had no choice. She cried and sobbed until there were no more tears. Lisa passed her some Kleenex and Madison blew her nose and dried her eyes. Lisa sat quietly beside her through it all and said nothing.

"Do you want to talk about it?" she asked, finally.

Madison realized it had been just that afternoon that Ashley had asked her the same question. But this time she couldn't talk about it. Not without getting Luke and Jennifer in trouble.

"No."

"That's okay, you don't have to. It's funny, though, when I saw you and Ashley together this afternoon I thought things were beginning to look up for you."

"They were," replied Madison. "But they're not anymore." There was a long pause before Madison continued. "In fact, I had two new friends and I blew it with both of them today. I'm such a loser." Madison realized how ironic it was that Ricky was mad at her for *not* telling Jennifer she was taking First Chair and Ashley was mad at her for telling Jennifer she *was* taking it.

"Do you mind me asking if this has something to do with the First Chair thing?" asked Lisa.

"Yeah, it does, sort of. But it's more complicated than that. Anyway, Jennifer knows you offered it to me."

"Oh. How did she take the news?"

"Not too well."

"I bet," laughed Lisa. "But perhaps it'll motivate her to work a little harder. Now she knows she's got competition."

They sat in comfortable silence for a few minutes.

"Do you really want to go home?" asked Lisa.

"Yes. But I guess I can finish out the week. And I've changed my mind. I would like to take First Chair." Madison couldn't let Jennifer off the hook, unpunished.

Lisa put her arm around Madison again and gave her a squeeze. "I'm proud of you. You've made the right decision. Now, help me douse the fire."

# Chapter Nine

In Madison's cabin, the girls discussed whether they should go after her. They decided against it, but sat on their beds, wondering where she had gone.

"Do you think we should at least tell someone that Madison's missing?" asked Danica.

"No," answered Kyla, Jennifer's friend. "Because then we would have to explain why she left and that would lead to her fight with Jennifer and we sure don't want to get into that."

"She could be wandering around out there in the dark," argued Ashley. "Something could happen to her and then we'd feel terrible."

"She's probably with Ed or Lisa right now, squealing on me," snarled Jennifer. "Don't worry about her. She can take care of herself."

The girls went to bed, but Ashley tossed and turned, listening to the sounds of the night. When she eventually heard footsteps approaching the cabin she flicked her flashlight on and beamed it on Madison's face as she entered the cabin.

"Are you okay?" she whispered.

"Yeah," answered Madison, and smiled at the look of concern on Ashley's face. "Don't worry. I didn't get eaten by a cougar," she added.

"I'm glad," answered Ashley. She kept her flashlight on until Madison had changed and climbed into bed. "Goodnight, Madison."

"Goodnight, Ashley." Madison smiled to herself in the dark. Ashley still cared about her.

Lisa tapped her baton on the music stand Tuesday morning.

"I have an announcement to make," she said. She waited until she had the attention of all the woodwind players. "As you know, Madison joined our band about ten months ago. During those ten months she has made incredible progress, so I have asked her to take First Chair."

There was complete silence in the room. Madison stared at the floor. Part of her felt smug—satisfied that she was punishing Jennifer for being with Luke. But part of her felt awkward and a little afraid. Would the other girls forgive her or would they shun her for bumping Jennifer from the position?

"You can change places now, girls," said Lisa. Madison carefully avoided looking at Jennifer as they traded places. She sensed her tension, though, and knew she hadn't heard the end of it from Jennifer.

As she walked slowly back toward the cabin after practice, Madison felt a slap on her back. She turned to see Ricky's beaming face.

"Way to go, Madison!" he said. "I knew you had it in you!"

"Thanks, Ricky," she answered, without enthusiasm.

"What's the matter?" he asked, but before she could answer Madison saw Kyla and Jennifer heading over to where they were standing. She turned to walk away, but Jennifer was too quick.

"Look at the lovebirds, Kyla. Don't they make a cute couple?"

"Leave Ricky out of this, Jennifer. If you have a problem you can talk to me about it."

"No problem, Madison. Just wondering where you got to last night. Maybe you and Ricky had a little rendezvous. Tell me. Where do you guys go to do it? In the forest? In the washrooms? Behind the hall?"

"What are you talking about, Jennifer?" Ricky looked puzzled.

"Just ignore her," answered Madison. She took his arm and tried to steer him around the girls but Jennifer moved to block their way.

"Did you squeal on Luke and me?" she asked. Madison knew that this was what was really bothering her.

"That's for me to know and you to find out," she answered. No use letting her off the hook too easily, she thought. "Come on, Ricky, let's shoot some baskets."

Jennifer and Kyla stood watching them on

the basketball court for a few minutes, but eventually left, heading in the direction of the cabin. When they were gone, Ricky held the ball still.

"What was that all about?" he asked. Madison considered telling him about the scene in the cabin the night before, but decided against it. Ricky would encourage her to report the incident and she didn't need him making her feel guilty again. How was he to know the real reason she couldn't report them? No matter what Luke did or said, Madison still liked him and didn't want to do anything to hurt him.

"Oh, she just can't admit to herself that I'm the better flute player," she lied. "She'll get over it. Pass me the ball."

Madison and Ricky shot baskets until the brass section finished its morning rehearsal. Out of the corner of her eye Madison saw Luke come out of the door and head down the ramp, swinging his trumpet case. When he spotted her and Ricky playing basketball, he stood and watched for a moment. Madison pretended she hadn't noticed him. After a few minutes he approached the court.

"Can I play too?" he asked.

Ricky looked at Madison, puzzled. Madison

shrugged her shoulders, acting cool but feeling her heart race. "Sure," Ricky answered eventually and tossed him the ball. They took turns taking shots at the hoop until Luke's friend, Andrew, came over and joined them. Soon there was a small crowd all shooting baskets, so Andrew organized teams and an informal game began. Madison played with the boys because she couldn't think of a discreet way out, but she quickly became breathless and hot. She plunked herself on the sidelines to watch. Ricky was doing his best to keep up with the older boys, but Madison could tell he was tiring, too.

When Luke noticed Madison sitting out, he went over and plopped himself down beside her. She pretended not to notice and kept on watching the game.

"Do you want to go for a walk?" he asked.

It was the last thing in the world Madison had expected him to say. Confused, she just nodded and got to her feet. She picked up her flute case, which was still sitting near the basketball court. As they walked away, Madison glanced back at the game. She saw Ricky watching them leave, surprise written all over his face.

"You deserve to be First Chair," said Luke,

breaking the awkward silence.

"Thanks," replied Madison. "I'm surprised to hear you saying that, though. Jennifer wouldn't be impressed."

"Just telling it like it is."

The awkward silence was back. They were walking along the edge of the forest, away from the cabins.

"Shall we walk in the woods where it's cooler?" he asked.

"You're really big on breaking the rules, aren't you," Madison replied.

"I'm hot."

"And Jennifer might see us together, right?" Madison hated sounding so bitter, but she didn't want him to think she was naive, either.

He didn't answer, just looked back toward the camp and then slipped in among the trees.

Looking back on it later, Madison didn't know why she followed him. If she had listened to the little voice in her head she would have turned around and gone back to camp. But when it came to Luke, Madison didn't want to listen to the little voice. So she found herself in the forbidden forest once again, alone with Luke. As she followed him through the trees she felt a wonderful sense of elation. She never would have guessed a week ago that she would be alone in the woods with Luke. She felt a little dizzy, a little disoriented. She knew he didn't feel the same way about her as she did about him. After all, he had been with Jennifer just last night, but right now Madison didn't care why Luke had asked her to go for a walk. She was happy just to be with him. Maybe he would get to know and like her and their friendship could turn into something more … something romantic.

The trees became a little less dense and Luke waited for Madison to come up beside him. They walked along in silence for a few minutes. The only sounds were the crunching of leaves beneath their feet and the chirping of birds far above their heads. Luke noticed a fallen tree that would make a good bench to sit on.

"Do you want to sit and talk for a bit?" he asked.

"Sure," she replied. She sat down and hugged her flute case to her chest, knowing how awkward she looked but helpless to change the situation. He sat beside her. She thought he would get to the point quickly, begging her once again not to squeal on him and Jennifer. But he sat quietly, listening to the forest sounds. Madison wondered if he felt as uncomfortable as she did. Eventually he looked at her and noticed the flute case that she still clutched nervously. His eyes lit up.

"Would you play that piece you composed again? It was cool."

This guy was full of surprises, thought Madison. First she had assumed he had brought her here to beg not to be reported to Ed. Then, when that didn't happen, she began to worry that it was going to be like Ashley said—they get you alone and then their hands—all over … She wondered how she would stop him. She thought back to the kiss she had witnessed last night. Hadn't she wished that it was her he was kissing?

Asking her to play the flute was the last thing she expected.

"Are you serious? You want me to play the flute? Here?"

"Yeah. Why not?"

"Someone from camp might hear me."

"We're way too far away. C'mon." He seemed more relaxed now that he had found some way to break the silence.

"Okay." Madison opened the case and assembled her flute. Lifting it to her mouth, she paused, focusing on the music she was about to play. She began, softly at first and then louder and more clearly as the music took over, the way it always did. Soon she forgot herself and just played, the music mingling with the forest sounds. As she played the last bittersweet note, she remembered where she was, and the warm feelings brought on by the music quickly disappeared. She glanced at Luke and found him staring at her, his expression unreadable. He seemed to be lost in thought, unaware that she had stopped playing.

Madison looked at her watch. "C'mon," she said. "We had better get back for lunch." She was relieved to have found a way to break the uncomfortable silence, but sorry that her time alone with Luke had to end. She hadn't found him arrogant or cocky, but reflective, sensitive. Life was full of surprises. She liked this Luke even better than the Luke she had imagined him to be. So good-looking—but sensitive and

vulnerable, too.

Luke put his hand on Madison's arm as she started to stand up. He looked nervous.

"Could you meet me here again later?" he asked.

"I guess so," she replied.

"Let's come separately this time. We're less likely to get caught. Do you think you can find this log again?"

"Yeah. I think so."

"Good." Luke led the way back to the camp through the trees. When they came to the edge of the forest he turned to her.

"See you later, then."

"Yeah, okay," was all she could say. "Later."

# Chapter Ten

Madison returned her flute case to the cabin and headed over to Spruce Hall for lunch. She saw Ashley approaching the hall from the direction of the beach.

"Wait up, Madison," Ashley hollered. When she caught up to Madison she asked, "Where did you go this morning? I was looking all over for you."

"I played basketball for a bit and then I just walked around," she lied. "Why?"

"I just wanted to apologize for the way I acted last night. I realize now that it was a personal thing, and you weren't ready to discuss it. But I'm really happy for you. You deserve to be First Chair."

"Thanks." They had selected their lunches and were sitting together at their cabin's usual table. It was still early and the other girls hadn't arrived yet. Madison felt flustered and excited about her morning walk with Luke and decided to confide in Ashley about what she had really done that this morning.

"I've got something to tell you, Ashley. But you've got to swear to keep it a secret."

"Sure. What is it?" Ashley leaned forward to hear Madison.

"I didn't just walk around this morning," she said. "I … "

"Hi, Madison. Hi, Ashley." Ricky was suddenly standing at the table, a big, friendly smile plastered on his face. "Can I join you?"

Madison sighed. "Sure," she said, moving her tray a little to make room for him. She looked at Ashley apologetically, hoping she'd understand and wait until later to talk. Ashley smiled back. She understood.

"Where'd you and Luke go this morning?" Ricky asked coolly.

He's jealous, Madison realized with a start. She glanced at Ashley. Ashley raised her eyebrows and Madison nodded. At least now, Ashley knew what they had to talk about.

"We just walked and talked. He wanted to congratulate me for taking First Chair."

"Huh," was all Ricky said. Madison suspected he didn't believe her, but she was grateful that he didn't press the point.

While they ate, Madison casually glanced around the hall, which was now filling up with campers. She spotted Luke and Jennifer discussing something privately in a corner. They looked unhappy and Jennifer seemed to be angry. They were probably trying to decide whether she had squealed on them or not. Or maybe Jennifer had heard that Luke had gone for a walk with her. Madison didn't care. She was meeting Luke again that afternoon, not Jennifer.

"Madison. Wake up!" Ashley waved a hand in front of Madison's face.

"Sorry. What did you say?"

"Ricky wants to know if we want to play badminton this afternoon."

"No, not today, thanks," she mumbled.

"Why not?" asked Ricky.

"I've made other plans," she answered. She realized Ashley was staring hard at her. She stared back, willing her to change the subject.

"I'll play, Ricky," said Ashley.

"Great," he said, but he couldn't mask his disappointment. He got up to leave. "I'll see you then, Ashley."

"Right."

As soon as he was gone, the other girls from their cabin descended on their table. They were full of chatter about their morning. Jennifer was the last to join them. By then Madison had finished her lunch, so she got up to leave as soon as Jennifer sat down. A hush fell over the table.

"Wait for me, Madison," said Ashley.

Madison realized that this was a big turning point in her relationship with Ashley. By deciding to leave with Madison instead of staying with the other girls, Ashley had publicly declared her friendship to Madison. Madison felt a huge wave of gratitude come over her as they left the hall.

"So where did you go with Luke this morning?" asked Ashley as they strolled around the camp.

"That's what I was just about to tell you when Ricky joined us," answered Madison. "I didn't want to discuss it with him."

"I figured that much," said Ashley.

"After practice this morning, I was talking to Ricky when Jennifer and Kyla started hassling us. I could tell that Jennifer just wanted to know if I had squealed on her. I didn't tell her that I hadn't. She still doesn't know one way or the other. Then Ricky and I started to shoot baskets, and Luke and his friends asked if they could join us."

"They did?" asked Ashley. The older campers and the younger campers rarely mixed.

"Yeah. We thought it was strange, too. Before we knew it a game was organized. I knew I was out of my league—those guys are so tall—so I sat down to watch. Ricky hung in there. Then Luke came over and asked me to go for a walk."

"Didn't you find that a bit suspicious?"

"Yeah. I thought he just wanted to know whether I had squealed on him and Jennifer. But he never asked me."

"Really! What did you talk about?"

"Not much. But get this. He asked me to play my flute for him."

"No way! Really?"

"Really. We were in the woods …"

"You went in the woods with him?"

"Yeah. Don't ask me why. And we were sitting on a log … I kept wondering what he wanted. And then he asked me to play the song I composed."

"Get real!" Ashley looked at Madison, wondering whether this was all just a big joke. Madison laughed at Ashley's incredulous expression.

"And that's not the weirdest part," she continued. "He asked me to meet him again after rest time."

"No way! In the woods again?"

"Yeah. Same place."

"Are you going to go?"

"Yeah, I said I would."

"But you can't go in the woods. You could get sent home. Or meet a cougar!"

"Well, I'm not too worried about cougars, and it's kinda funny, just last night I was begging Lisa to send me home."

Ashley looked at Madison. "Do you still want to go home?" she asked gently.

Madison returned the look. Quietly she said, "No. Not now that I know you're my friend." Ashley smiled back. Then Madison continued, "But I think I will meet Luke. My curiosity is killing me."

Ashley didn't respond, but she looked un-happy. They headed back to the cabin for rest time.

# Chapter Eleven

Madison looked back quickly before she entered the woods. People were used to her wandering around alone, but she didn't want anyone to see her entering the forest. Once under the trees, her confidence began to waver. This morning, with Luke leading the way, the forest had seemed friendly, cool and accepting. Now it seemed oddly quiet and threatening. She hesitated, wondering whether she should turn back. But then she thought of Luke. She needed to know what he wanted. His intentions couldn't be bad. After all, he had asked her to play her music. It must affect him the same way it affected her. Maybe he just wanted to get to know the girl behind the music better and, being older, he didn't want to pursue this relationship with her, a junior girl, in front of his friends. Their teasing would be too humiliating. Madison forged on.

As she neared the clearing with the log-bench, Madison suddenly became aware of the sound of voices. She hesitated, straining to hear better. Was it Luke? Who was he talking to? Had he been caught in the woods by a counselor? She wasn't close enough to identify the voices or to hear what they were saying, but she knew she'd better be careful. Slowly, very carefully, she crept toward the clearing. The forest was dense enough that she could stay hidden behind the large trees but still get close to the clearing un-detected. She was startled to hear a female voice.

"We wouldn't have to be here if you had said what you were supposed to say this morning, so don't whine to me about missing your tennis game!" Madison sucked in her breath when she realized it was Jennifer's voice, raised in anger.

"I tried to lay it on the line for her, but I just couldn't. She looked so trusting. I just couldn't do it."

Madison's heart was racing now. It was Luke that Jennifer was having this heated conversation with, and they were talking about her. She strained to hear better. What was it that Luke was supposed to "lay on the line" for her? Why was Jennifer here? What were they up to?

"Don't you realize that once you had her in the woods, she was breaking the rules just as much as we did last night? I thought you got the picture. She'd be sent home for being here just as we'd be sent home for being in the cabin last night. So she wouldn't squeal. She'd be as guilty as us. Simple."

"You don't need to talk to me like I'm stupid, Jennifer!" Madison could hear anger building in Luke's voice now. "I told you. She's a sweet kid and she won't squeal—I'm sure of it. I don't like confronting her like this."

Madison's head was spinning. So that was it. Blackmail. Luke was supposed to get Madison to break the rules so they would be even. Her initial reaction was anger mixed with humiliation. Trust Jennifer to hatch a scheme like this. But Luke's last comment softened Madison's anger. Luke had called her a "sweet kid" and he trusted her not to squeal. In fact, he liked her

so much he hadn't had the nerve to go through
with the blackmail—the first time. Madison considered her options. Should she quietly sneak
back the way she had come and tell Luke, later,
that she had changed her mind about meeting
him, or should she step forward now and have
it out with Jennifer? She could tell Jennifer that
she didn't have anything to lose—that she didn't
care if she got sent home—she didn't like Band
Camp anyway. But Madison knew she would be
bluffing. She had finally made a real friend, and
she didn't really want to be sent home. Arguing
with Jennifer wouldn't prove anything. Best to
sneak back the way she had come and let them
wonder. She would be in control of the situation.

A twig snapped nearby.

"Madison, is that you?" Jennifer called into
the thick forest. There was no reply. From her
position behind a large tree Madison could see
Luke and Jennifer peering into the woods,
somewhere to her left. She stood perfectly still
and watched the expressions on their faces
change from puzzlement to horror. Madison
turned to see what they were looking at and almost jumped out of her skin. A sleek, golden-
eyed cougar stood staring at her, its only

movement the twitching of the very end of its tail. The cat, which Madison assumed was one of the orphaned kittens, looked as startled as she felt. They watched each other for a few moments. Madison, realizing the animal was experiencing the same fear she was—it was clear from the expression in its eyes—was immobilized by terror. Her feet felt glued to the ground; she couldn't muster up a yelp, let alone a scream. But when the cat finally moved, squatting down as though about to pounce, Madison suddenly found her feet unglued and bounded into the clearing with Luke and Jennifer. They jumped when they saw her, unaware that it was her the cat had been watching. The cat followed her move with its eyes, but remained crouched.

"Where did you come from?" asked Jennifer, not taking her eyes off the cougar.

"The woods, obviously," answered Madison, her eyes fixed on the cougar as well. "What should we do?" she asked. "Do you think it will attack?"

"Remember what Ed told us," said Luke. "Cougars only attack if they're starving, sick or provoked." He spoke in a quiet monotone, trying not to excite the wild animal. "He looks perfectly healthy and hopefully he's not starving, so if we don't provoke him we'll be okay."

Jennifer reached down and picked up a large stick lying on the ground at their feet.

"One of us could chase it with this," she suggested.

"What do you think provoking means?" asked Luke, scornfully.

"Well, maybe if we all charge it at once it will run off," suggested Jennifer.

"No," said Madison firmly. "Stand still. Don't move."

The cat was still crouching, motionless except for the slow flick of its tail. Madison, Jennifer and Luke stood equally still for what seemed an eternity. Then Madison thought she saw the cougar relax, the fear leaving its eyes. It stood up and looked to the left.

"Stay still," she said again. "It's going to leave."

The cougar began to pick its way into the woods, away from the campers. Madison felt herself begin to breathe again. She could sense the tension leaving Luke and Jennifer, too.

"It's leaving," whispered Jennifer. "We're okay." But suddenly there were new sounds in the woods. Voices approaching them, arguing.

"This is stupid, Ricky. We don't know where we're going. They could be anywhere."

Madison froze again. It was Ashley's voice. She and Ricky must have followed Madison into the woods. She saw the cougar pause and peer into the trees, looking for the source of the voices. Then it looked back at the group still standing motionless in the clearing. Madison could see the look of fear returning to its eyes. The cougar crouched, its ears flattened against its head and its black-tipped tail whipping back and forth. It feels cornered, she thought. The cat snarled at the sound of people approaching through the trees. Madison realized she had to warn Ashley and Ricky before they stumbled right into it. She caught a glimpse of Ashley's bright pink T-shirt through the thick woods. They were headed right toward the cougar.

"Ashley, is that you?" she hollered.

"Madison! Where are you?"

"Straight ahead. But don't come any further. There's a cougar between us."

"This is great. Just great," complained Jennifer. "It's a regular party in here now." She was still holding the stick.

"Keep your cool, Jennifer," warned Luke. "He'll go if we just leave him alone."

"Well, I'm getting a little tired of this," she answered. "I think we need to hurry him on his way." She raised the stick above her head and stepped aggressively toward the cougar. "Shoo!" she shouted at the cat. "Get lost! Move it!"

The startled cat turned to face Jennifer as she moved forward, baring its front teeth and hissing, warning her to keep her distance. But Jennifer kept moving, swinging her stick.

"Jennifer! Stop it!" ordered Madison.

"What's going on Madison?" Ashley yelled through the trees. The cougar turned to see where the voice was coming from. Jennifer took a few more steps. Madison could see that the cougar was starting to panic, feeling trapped, knowing there were people behind it in the woods and Jennifer approaching with her stick swinging. Crouching again, the cougar turned its head from Jennifer to the invisible threat approaching through the trees.

"Jennifer, back off now!" ordered Luke. He moved forward, grabbing her arm, but the cougar must have thought Luke was acting aggressively, too. It was the final straw. With a wild screech, the cat leapt into the air, landing close to Jennifer and Luke. Madison screamed, momentarily distracting the cougar's attention from Luke and Jennifer.

"Ricky, Ashley!" she screamed. "Run for help, fast!"

Later, Madison's recollection of what followed was only a blur. She remembered screams, her own mixed with Luke's and Jennifer's. She remembered golden fur and human skin all tangled together, and then blood. Blood seemed to be everywhere. The cougar knocked both Luke and Jennifer down in one bound, but then had to deal with two people kicking and struggling. Glancing about, Madison spotted a large rock. She picked it up and moved closer to the struggle. By then Luke had freed himself and was trying to distract the cougar, which had a screaming Jennifer pinned to the ground. Waiting for just the right moment, Madison threw the rock at the young cougar's head, praying silently that her aim wouldn't be off and hit Jennifer instead. But it hit the cougar, stunning it slightly and giving Jennifer time to roll away from its grip. Madison and Luke were quickly at her side, dragging her away from the angry, frightened cat. By the time it had regained its composure, Madison and Luke had pulled Jennifer some distance away, and were watching it quietly. It stared back at them, obviously trying to make some kind of a decision. From this distance, Madison could see that the animal wasn't nearly as big as its mother had been. It was just a young and frightened cat that didn't know how to handle this situation. Madison knew she had to soothe it somehow, so she began to talk to it in a quiet, calm voice. It watched her, ears cocked forward. She kept talking. She told it that they weren't going to hurt it. That everything would be okay. That it was a good cat.

It worked. With a little growl, the cougar turned and soundlessly padded away into the forest, looking back a couple of times. As frightened as she was, Madison found herself feeling sorry for it.

"I'm bleeding," wailed Jennifer. "Do something!"

Madison glanced down at Jennifer, still lying on the ground where they had dragged her. She glanced at Luke. Both were bleeding, but Jennifer seemed to have the more serious injuries. She squatted next to Jennifer, who was beginning to wail hysterically. She was sweating and shaking. Her face was ashen. Madison wondered if she had gone into shock.

*Stop the bleeding. Stop the bleeding.* A little voice in Madison's mind reminded her of her first-aid training, taken two years ago at a baby-sitters' preparation course. What could she use? She had on only a T-shirt and shorts. She looked at Luke. His T-shirt was already blood soaked, but it would have to do.

"Take off your shirt and rip it into strips," she ordered. He looked as confused as the cougar had when she hit it with the rock. "Now! Quickly!" Luke did as he was told, and Madison wrapped the strips around Jennifer's cuts that seemed to be bleeding the most. Then she turned her attention to Luke. He was just standing there, watching her. He must be in shock too, she figured.

"Sit here, Luke," she said gently, steering him over to the log they had sat on together just that morning. With the remaining strips of T-shirt she tended to his worst injuries. They were both going to require a lot of stitches, she thought. She showed Luke how to use his hands to put pressure on the remaining gashes. Jennifer's wails had subsided to little sobs. Madison returned to talk to her. Her eyes were closed and the shaking had become violent. Madison was afraid she was going to slip into unconsciousness. She had to keep her awake.

"Ashley and Ricky will be back with help any second now," she told Jennifer. "Hang in there. It's not far back to camp. You're going to be fine."

For the next ten minutes, Madison moved back and forth between Luke and Jennifer, trying to keep their spirits up and assessing whether the bleeding had stopped or not. Eventually she heard her name being called through the woods.

"Over here," she answered. "We're over here."

Ricky and Ashley were back, bringing Lisa and Ed with them. Ed had a walkie-talkie with him, and as soon as he saw the situation he called back to the camp and told a counselor to arrange for paramedics to be helicoptered into the camp. He lifted Jennifer in his arms and led the procession back through the woods to the camp. Lisa took Luke's arm and coaxed him along. Ashley and Ricky each took one of Madison's hands and they followed the others. Now that help was here and she no longer had to take charge, Madison felt strangely weak. She allowed herself to be led back to the camp, feeling more nauseated by the minute. As soon as they got there she made a mad dash for the washroom, where she was violently ill. Ashley waited at the sink and handed her a cold washcloth when she was done.

"You okay, Madison?" she asked. They were the first words they had spoken.

"Yeah. I think so." She glanced at herself in the mirror. She was spattered with blood, and her face was pale. "What were you and Ricky doing in the woods, anyway?"

Ashley hesitated before answering. "I was worried about you. I didn't trust Luke, so I told Ricky what was going on and he thought we better go find you."

"Good thing you did."

"Yeah, as it turns out." There was a long silence in the washroom. "Ed is waiting to see you."

"Thanks, Ashley. I'm sorry to cause so much trouble."

"I'm just glad you're okay."

# Chapter Twelve

Madison waited in the wings to make her entrance onto the stage. It was Saturday night, the last night of Band Camp. With Jennifer in the hospital recuperating from the cougar attack, Madison had taken on the lead in her cabin's skit. The stage was decorated to look like the waiting room in a dental office. Madison wandered onto the stage, chewing gum and blowing big bubbles. She took a seat and picked up a magazine. She continued to chew until Ashley, dressed as a nurse, came onto the stage.

"The dentist will see you now, dear," said

Nurse Ashley in a hilarious nasal whine. "But no gum, please."

Nurse Ashley left the stage and Madison looked around for somewhere to put her gum. She pretended to put it on the arm of her chair, and headed offstage. There was a chuckle from the audience. Danica came onstage next. Picking up the magazine, she sat down in the same chair. When Nurse Ashley called her in to see the dentist, she found her arm stuck to the wad of gum. With a scowl, she pulled it off and pretended to throw it on the floor. Alicia came onstage next and stepped on the gum. With great difficulty she removed it and left it on the seat of the chair. One by one, the other girls came onto the stage and dealt with the invisible gum. Marisa sat on it and put on a wonderful performance trying to get it off the seat of her shorts. She stuck it on the wall for Sarah to lean on. Sarah unstuck herself and placed it on a magazine cover, and Kyla got it stuck to her blouse as she read the magazine. Finally, Kyla left it stuck to the arm of the chair once more. Madison came back onstage, picked the gum off the arm of the chair and popped it back into her mouth. The crowd roared as she chomped on the pretend gum and skipped offstage.

"Excellent acting, Madison!" congratulated Danica. The girls were backstage enjoying the sound of the applause coming from the audience.

"You too, Danica," replied Madison. "Everyone was great." They stood around for a few more minutes chatting about their performance.

"Come on, you guys. Let's go find some seats. The next skit's about to start." Madison led the way into the hall and to their row of empty seats. Ever since the cougar incident the girls had treated her differently, expecting her to be the leader. When Ed had described the scene in the forest to the campers, Madison was portrayed as the hero. He told of how she had thrown the rock at the cougar's head, stunning it so she could rescue Jennifer from its vicious claws, and how she'd then calmed the young animal with her voice. Madison hadn't tried to explain that it was her fear that had actually taken over, and that she had thrown the rock to save her own life, not necessarily Jennifer's. She had told the truth, though, about why they were in the forbidden forest and what had happened there, but Ed hadn't punished her. He must have felt she had suffered enough. She could have gone home, but she had chosen to stay. Jennifer was going to be okay, even though she was covered in stitches and her doctor needed to monitor her in case of infection. Luke also had received a lot of stitches, but his doctor had allowed him to come back to camp as long as he stayed clean and took it easy.

Madison watched as Luke performed his part in the skit. Except for the bandages covering the stitches on his arms, he looked unscathed by the cougar attack. Once again he looked confident and charming. But now Madison realized there was more to Luke than his self-assured good looks. She knew there was a hint of shyness in his character and that he was a decent person who hadn't wanted to hurt her, even when it was to his advantage. She knew he had common sense during times of danger. She had also figured out that he was too old for her; he would be graduating from high school in less than a year and would be out making his way in the world. But Madison didn't mind. They were friends now, and Luke treated her like a special sister. Ricky, on the other hand, was the same age as Madison and she knew he cared a lot for her. He had broken camp rules twice to protect her, and he and Ashley had come to her rescue in the woods. Now that she had gotten over her infatuation with Luke, she was beginning to find Ricky more interesting. She could relax with him. He wouldn't ask her to do anything she was uncomfortable with.

The curfew was lifted for the final campfire of Band Camp. Madison sat between Ashley and Ricky. As Ed lit the fire, she thought about her first few days here. Back then she wouldn't even come to the evening campfire, and she had spent her days wandering around the camp alone. Now she wished that camp would last another couple of weeks.

"I have a surprise snack for our final evening," announced Ed. "See if you can guess what it is."

"S'mores," shouted a chorus of voices.

"No."

"Wieners," called out Andrew.

"Marshmallows?"

"Nope. Give up?" asked Ed. The campers nodded.

"Beans on toast, of course," replied Ed. There was applause and laughter as Ed opened up a few jumbo-sized cans of beans and pulled bread out of his brown grocery bag. They toasted the bread over the fire while the beans were warmed in a large, cast-iron pot. Plates and cutlery were passed around and Ed dished out the beans. There was a warm feeling of community around the fire as the campers ate their snack and sipped hot chocolate.

After the usual campfire songs, Ed interrupted the festivities once more.

"The Beans on Toast Committee has an announcement to make," he said. Luke and his fellow committee members gathered on a log at one side of the fire. Andrew spoke first.

"The committee met this afternoon to decide what to do with the Beans on Toast Award plaque until next year," he said. "And we came to a unanimous decision." He looked around the group for permission to continue. The boys nodded for him to go on. "We feel there is a person here who has risen above and beyond the standard used for earning this prestigious award." He paused while the campers chuckled. "We would like to honor this person by asking them to guard this plaque with their life over the coming year. If they should fail in this duty, they will have to deal with the fury of this committee next year." He looked at Luke. "I think it would be fitting for Luke, our helpless cougar victim, to present this award." Luke rolled his eyes but laughed at Andrew's description of him. He took the plaque from Andrew and waited until the crowd was quiet again.

"The Keeper of the Plaque, as she is to be known from this day forward, is, of course, Madison Turner, the brave cougar fighter!"

The crowd came to its feet clapping, whistling and cheering as Madison made her way up to the impromptu stage. Her heart was pounding so hard she thought it would burst right through her chest. As she took the plaque from Luke, their eyes met. He was smiling his warm, big-brother smile. She smiled back. She knew she'd never forget this moment. She held the plaque over her head and looked at the faces of her friends and fellow band members as they clapped and cheered for her. She could hear Ricky cheering the loudest of all.

Shelley Hrdlitschka tries to live by the following quote from Margaret Mead: *"Never doubt that a small group of thoughtful, committed citizens can change the world; indeed, it is the only thing that ever has."*

A teacher for a number of years, Shelley discovered her love of children's literature during the daily storytime. Born and raised in Vancouver, Shelley now lives in Surrey, B.C. and is working on her second novel, *Disconnected,* which will be published by Orca Book Publishers in the fall of 1998.

Shelley is a member of various writing organizations, including CANSCAIP, CWILL and the Vancouver Children's Literature Roundtable. *Beans on Toast* is her first novel.

*More books for young readers from Orca Book Publishers*

**Brad's Universe** by Mary Woodbury
1-55143-120-3; $8.95 (cdn), $7.95(us); ages 12 to 16

**Cougar Cove** by Julie Lawson
1-55143-072-X; $7.95(cdn), $6.95(us); ages 8 to 11

**Draugr** by Arthur G. Slade
1-55143-094-0; $7.95(cdn), $6.95(us); ages 8 to 12

**A Fly Named Alfred** by Don Trembath
1-55143-083-5, $7.95(cdn), $6.95(us); ages 12 to 16

**A Light in the Dunes** by martha attema
1-55143-085-1; $7.95(cdn), $6.95(us); ages 11 to 14

**Skateway to Freedom** by Ann Alma
0-920501-89-3; $6.95(cdn), $5.95(us); ages 7 to 10

**Something Weird is Going On** by Christie Harris
1-55143-022-3; $6.95(cdn), $5.95(us); ages 8 to 11

**Summer of Madness** by Marion Crook
1-55143-041-X; $7.95(cdn), $6.95(us); ages 12 to 16

**Three Against Time** by Margaret Taylor
1-55143-067-3; $7.95(cdn), $6.95(us); ages 8 to 12

**A Time to Choose** by martha attema
1-55143-045-2; $7.95(cdn), $6.95(us); ages 11 to 14

**The Tuesday Cafe** by Don Trembath
1-55143-074-6; $7.95(cdn), $6.95(us); ages 12 to 16

**War of the Eagles** by Eric Walters
1-55143-099-1; $8.95(cdn), $7.95(us); ages 12 to 16

*For a complete list of books available through Orca Book Publishers, please call 1-800-210-5277.*